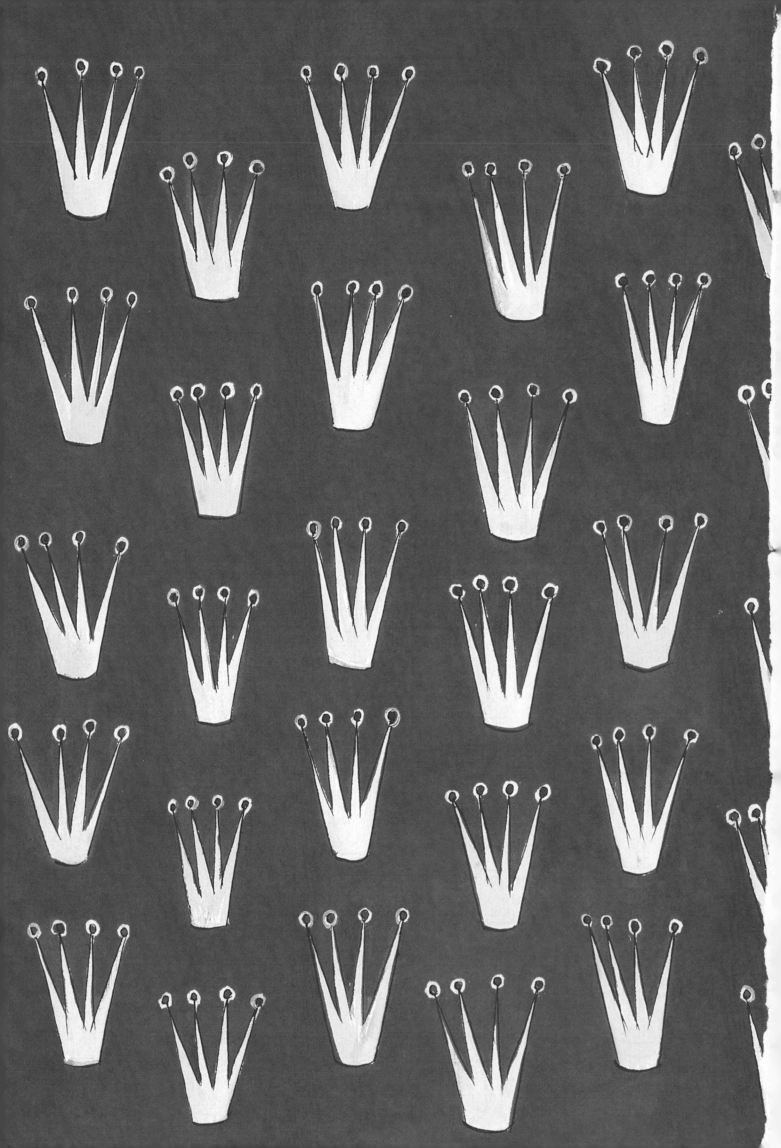

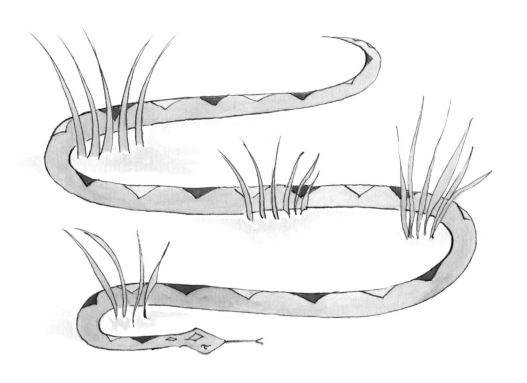

For Uncle Sam

GREENLEAF
BOOK GROUP PRESS

# The Lying King

## -Alex Beard-

There once was a king
who liked to tell lies.

He said it was day
beneath the night skies.

When it was wet,
he said it was dry.

He bragged about
how high he could fly.

And though the tales
he told were tall,
at the beginning
they started off small.

Before he was king
he lied to feel big,
a runt who wanted
to be a huge pig.

He said he was great
at whatever he tried.

"Tremendous! Outstanding!"
and "Splendid!" he cried.

And while such behavior was
thought of quite badly,
what could be done more
than think on it sadly?

"I am sooooo handsome,
and you are
sooooo ugly."

For as he grew older,
his fibbing got bolder.
The lies told to bully,
to prop him up fully.

And when the time came
for a new king to rise...

the warthog climbed up
on the backs of his lies.

"...much more kingly than you!"

'Til even the mighty
bent down to kneel,
under the weight
of the liar's zeal.

Now firm and in power,
his goals took a turn.
The king lied to steal
what he didn't earn.
He called the most honest
"Cheaters!" and worse...

"Thief!"

all the while padding
his own golden purse.

And even though many
thought him a lout,
too few spoke up
to call his lies out.

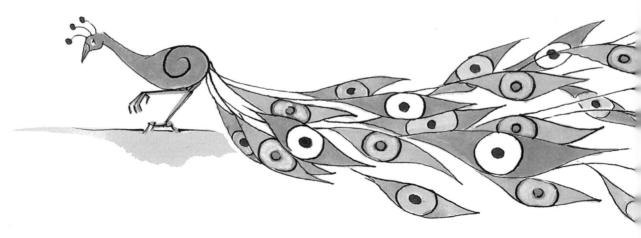

It's hard after all
to stand up to clout.

"Quiet,
Pipsqueak!"

"But Peacock is pretty,
and you're a warthog."

And so, much emboldened
with dishonest might...

the king called into question
all that was right.

"... and Yesterday
is Tomorrow."

He turned loyal subjects
against one another,
by making each question
the aims of the other.

'Til no one was certain
whom they could trust,
who might be righteous,
and who was unjust.

"Which Are You?"

In the confusion
the king got his way,
the lies a distraction
to hide his foul play.

And that's how he ruled
from his ill-gotten seat,
his kingdom secured
by doubt and deceit.

And his lies kept on going...

"No, no, no, no...
Tigers are Vegetarian.

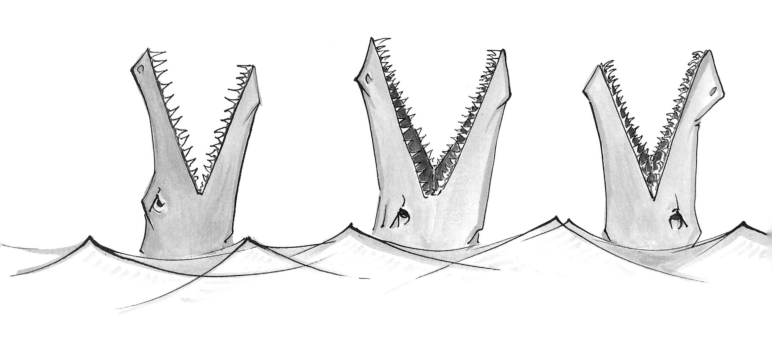

Like a river keeps flowing...

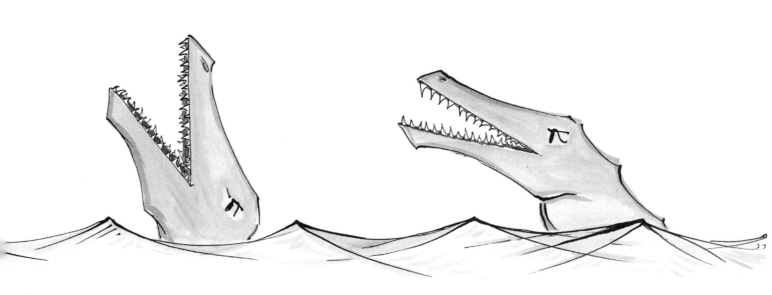

'Til nothing was safe,
no subject taboo,

"X#//@X∅#!"

and all that was false
was spoken as true.

That's when the lies
ensnared the king, too!

For once what was true
was turned on its head
and all that was right,
wrong instead...

...no one believed
a word the king said.

"I am the king!"
He screamed, and he spat.
But who could be certain
of something like that?

He gave out commands to "Do as I say!"

But all of his subjects had since turned away.

And so in the face of his numerous lies,
the animals finally opened their eyes.
They came to agree on a single true thing...

A lying pig should not be the king.

What happened next
took place quite quickly.

In ways that were pointed
(and a bit prickly!).

The warthog was banished,
expelled from his throne,
and sent far away
to live all alone,
where the only ones left
to hear his foul lies
were stinging mosquitos
and biting black flies.

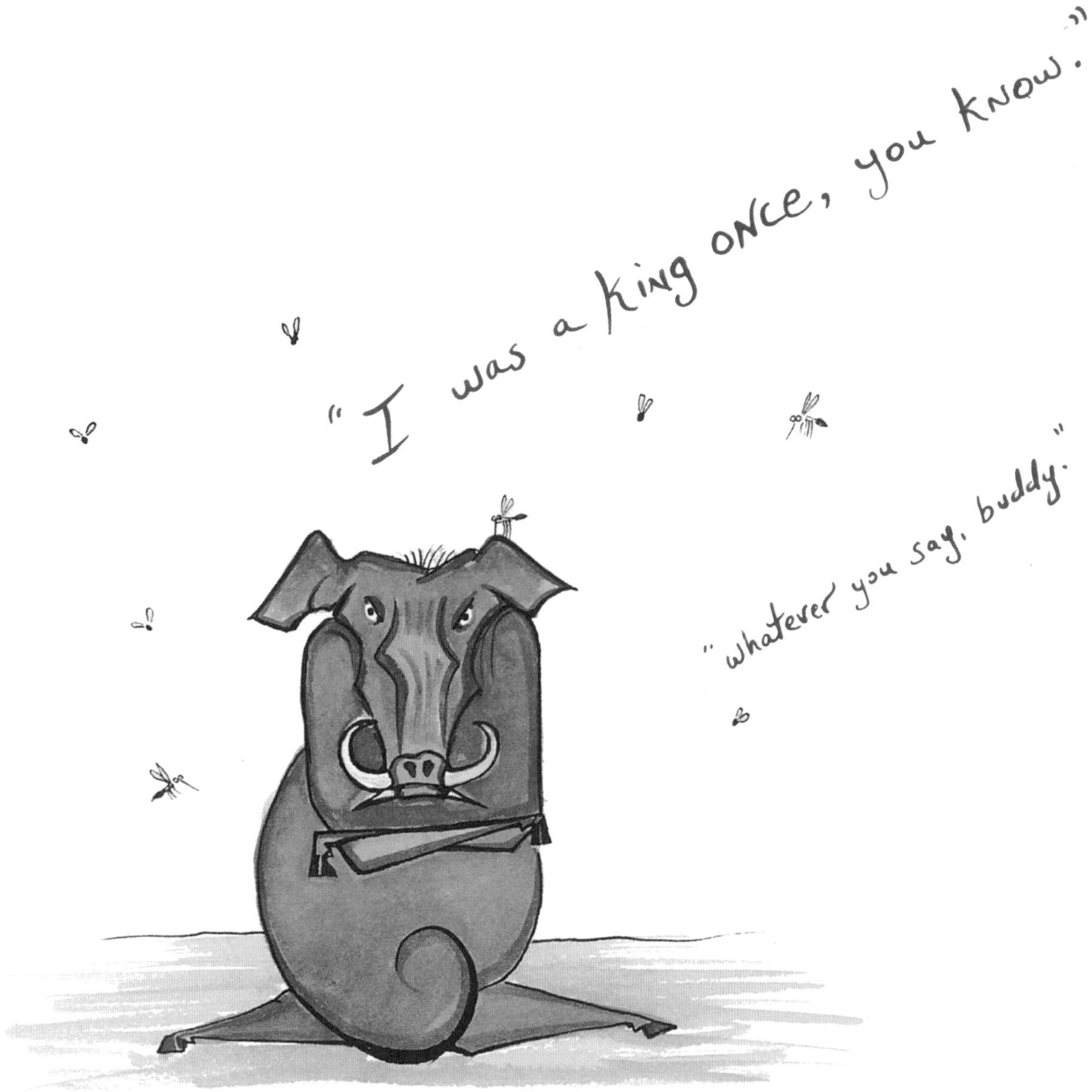
"I was a king once, you know."
"whatever you say, buddy."

'Cause that's in the end
how it always goes down...

The king who tells lies
loses his crown.

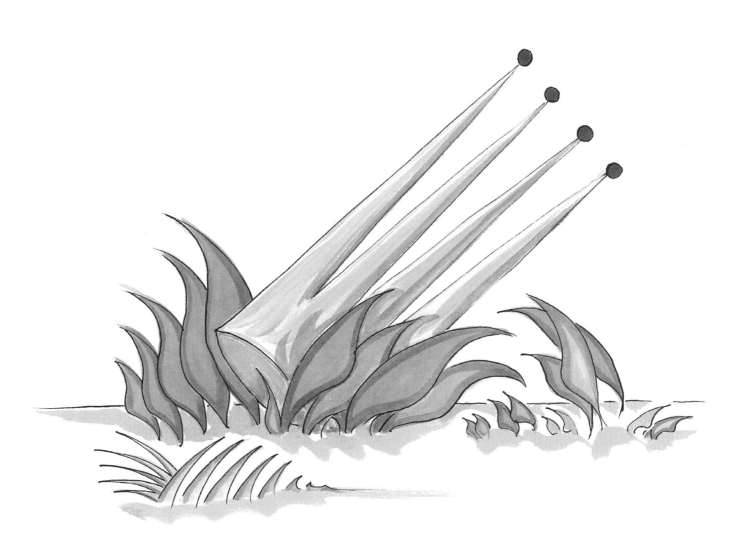

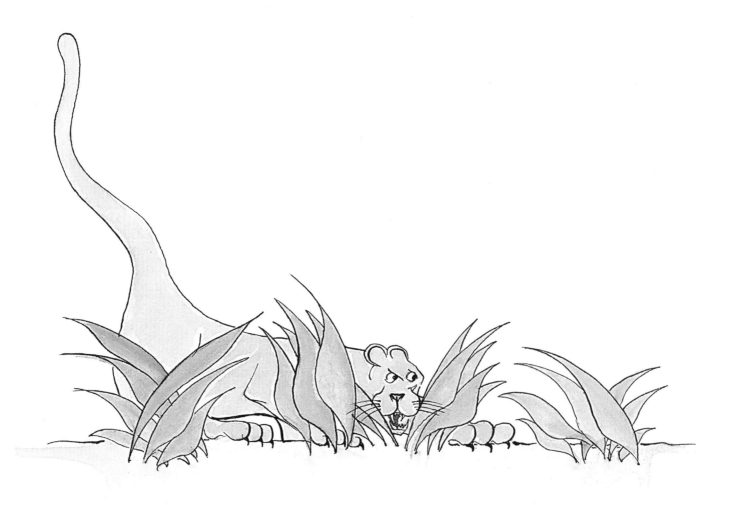

## ALEX BEARD

Alex Beard is an artist and author. He lives in New Orleans' Garden District in The Pink Elephant with his wife and two children, two dogs, a cat, three turtles, a hedgehog, and a pair of finches.

Published by Greenleaf Book Group Press
Austin, Texas
www.gbgpress.com

Distributed by Greenleaf Book Group

For ordering information or special discounts for bulk purchases, please contact Greenleaf Book Group at PO Box 91869, Austin, TX 78709, 512.891.6100.

Design and composition by Alex Beard and Greenleaf Book Group
Cover design and illustrations by Alex Beard

Publisher's Cataloging-in-Publication data is available.

Print ISBN: 978-1-62634-528-7

Part of the Tree Neutral® program, which offsets the number of trees consumed in the production and printing of this book by taking proactive steps, such as planting trees in direct proportion to the number of trees used: www.treeneutral.com

Manufactured through Asia Pacific Offset on acid-free paper
Manufactured in China
Q17110066

18 19 20 21 22 23    10 9 8 7 6 5 4 3 2 1

First Edition

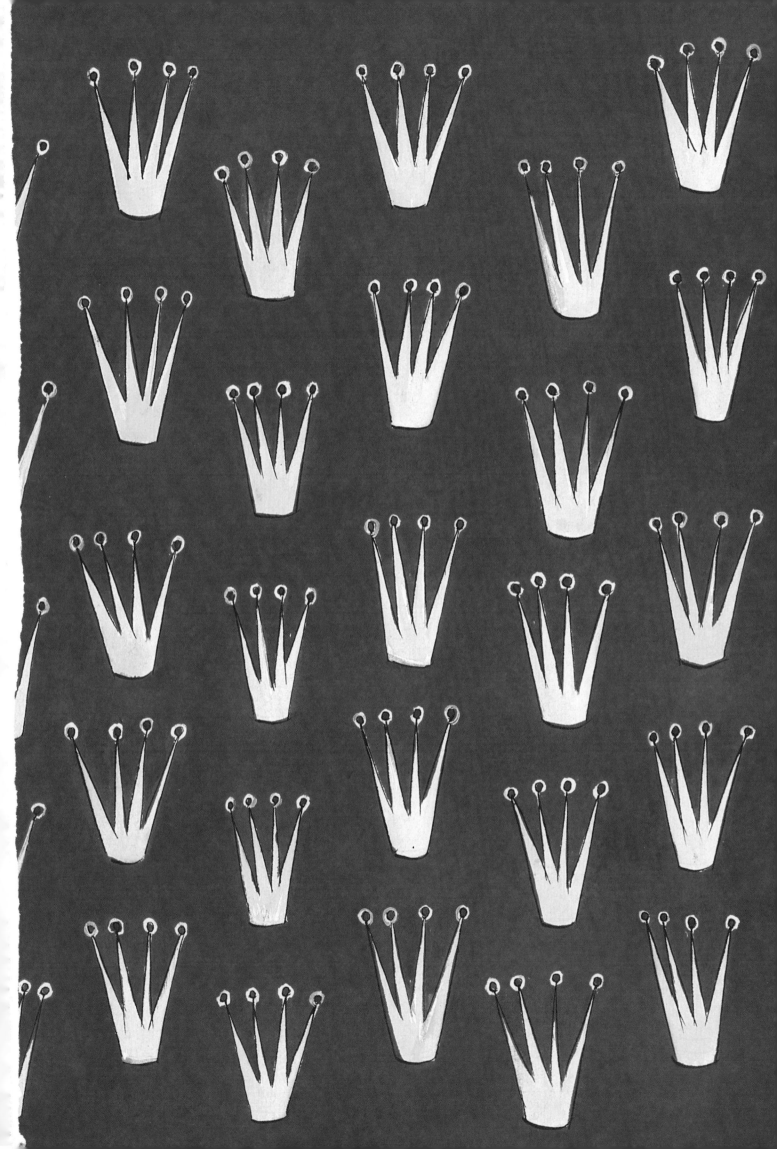

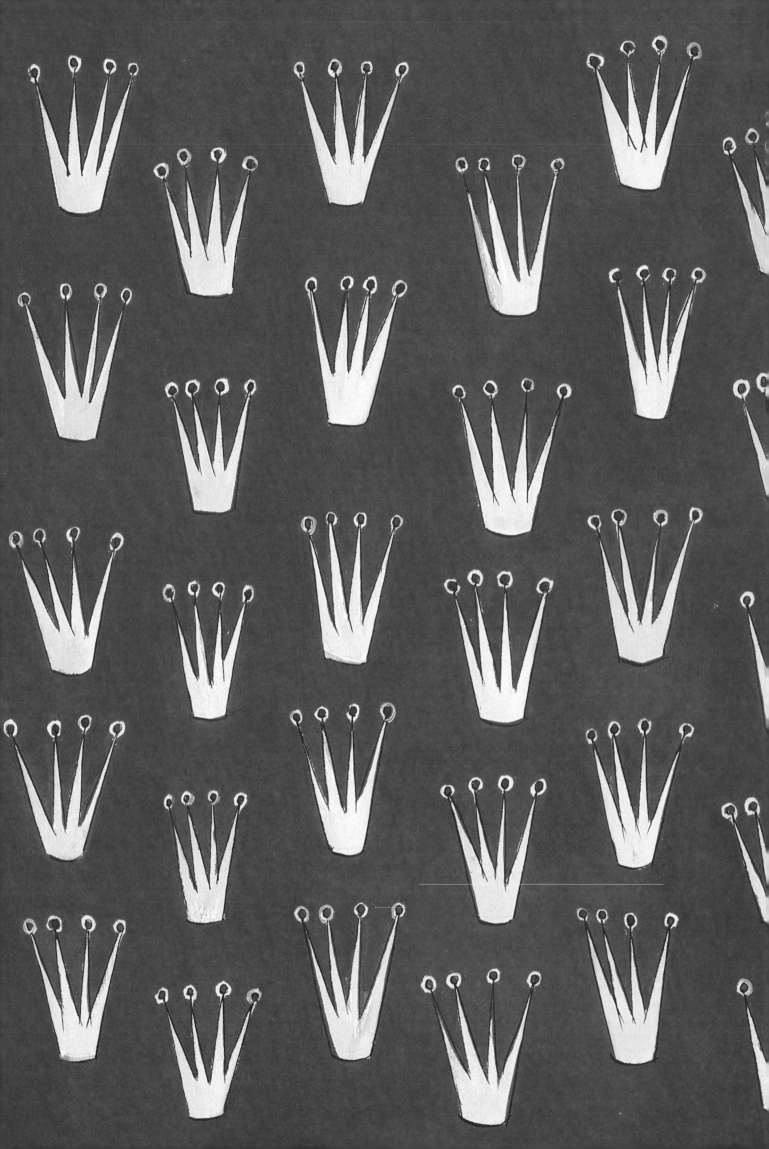